BUILDERS OF MODERN INDIA

RobinAge
Weekly Children's Newspaper

Illustrated by
Aditya Krishnamurth

SCHOLASTIC
New York Toronto London Auckland
Sydney New Delhi Hong Kong

Published by Scholastic India Pvt. Ltd.
A subsidiary of Scholastic Inc., New York, 10012 (USA).
Publishers since 1920, with international operations in Canada, Australia, New Zealand, the United Kingdom, India, and Hong Kong.

For information regarding permission, write to:
Scholastic India Pvt. Ltd.
A-27, Ground Floor, Bharti Sigma Centre
Infocity-1, Sector 34, Gurgaon-122001 (India)

First edition: June 2019
This reprinted edition, February 2026

ISBN-13: 978-93-5275-790-9

Printed at Shree Maitrey Printech Pvt. Ltd., Noida

Contents

AVUL PAKIR JAINULABDEEN ABDUL KALAM

15 October 1931 - 27 July 2015

Birthplace: Rameswaram, Tamil Nadu

Claim to Fame: Former president and 'Missile Man of India'

*'Learning gives creativity.
Creativity leads to thinking.
Thinking provides knowledge.
Knowledge makes you great.'*

A P J ABDUL KALAM

Aeronautical Engineer

Avul Pakir Jainulabdeen Abdul Kalam, better known as A P J Abdul Kalam, was the eleventh president of India. He was born on 15 October 1931 in Rameswaram, Tamil Nadu. Kalam hailed from a modest Muslim family and found success through hard work, determination and a deep sense of righteousness.

Kalam started working at the age of ten, when he sold newspapers to support his family financially. He claimed to have learnt spirituality from his father, compassion and benevolence from his mother and respect for discipline and hard work from his teachers. Despite the environment in which he grew up, which was dominated by religious fervour, sub-divisions and discrimination, he developed a positive attitude and respect for universal truths.

Of Flying Birds and Planes

Kalam was an average student in school and he loved mathematics. He studied at Schwartz Higher Secondary School, Ramanathapuram and then graduated from Saint Joseph's College, Tiruchirappalli in 1954. Inspired by an early teacher who introduced him to the study of flying birds, he pursued aeronautical engineering from the Madras Institute of Technology. He wanted to become a fighter pilot but his dream could not be fulfilled as there were only eight positions available in the Indian Air Force and he secured the ninth place in the qualifying exams.

In 1958, Kalam joined the Defence Research and Development Organisation (DRDO). He also worked under the eminent space scientist Vikram Sarabhai while he was part of the Indian National Committee for Space Research (INCOSPAR). INCOSPAR eventually became the Indian Space Research Organisation (ISRO) in 1969.

At ISRO, Kalam was a project director for SLV-III, India's indigenously designed and produced satellite launch vehicle. During his time at ISRO, Kalam also worked on many successful missiles like Agni, Prithvi, Akash, Trishul and Nag, which earned him the title, 'Missile Man of India'. Overall, Kalam spent more than forty years as a science administrator and scientist at DRDO and ISRO.

Kalam started working at the age of ten, when he sold newspapers to support his family financially.

From 1992 to 1997, Kalam served as the scientific advisor to the defence minister and in 1998, he played a prominent role in the Pokhran-II nuclear tests. In the same year, he put forth a plan called Technology Vision 2020, which was a road map to transform India into an advanced country. The plan included measures to increase agricultural productivity via technology and improve healthcare and education. In July 2002, Kalam was sworn in as India's eleventh president. Even as president, he remained dedicated to his love for science.

Soul of a Giver

Apart from his contributions to science, Kalam was known for his charity work. In fact, he formed a trust named PURA (Providing Urban Amenities to Rural Areas) to which he donated his presidential salaries when he became aware that the government takes care of its presidents. He also wrote many books, one of the most popular being *Wings of Fire*. He believed in dreaming big and acquiring knowledge and these views reflected in his writing and speeches.

Kalam received the Padma Bhushan in 1981, the Padma Vibhushan in 1990 and India's highest civilian honour, the Bharat Ratna, in 1997. He was also the recipient of the Veer Savarkar Award in 1998. In 2000, he was bestowed with the Ramanujan Award by the Alwars Research Centre. In 2007, he received the King Charles II Medal from the Royal Society, UK and in 2008, he received the prestigious Hoover Medal. In his honour, the government of Tamil Nadu created a Dr A P J Abdul Kalam Award, which is given to individuals who promote science, student welfare and the humanities. His birthday is celebrated as Youth Renaissance Day.

Even after Kalam retired, he continued to encourage the youth and gave many speeches to school and college students. In fact, he passed away while delivering one such speech on 27 July 2015.

CHARLES MARK CORREA

1 September 1930 - 16 June 2015

Birthplace: Secunderabad, Telangana

Claim to Fame: Iconic modern architect

'[The] complex and ambiguous relationship between man and nature is central to Indian architecture.'

CHARLES CORREA

Architect

Charles Mark Correa was an Indian architect, urban planner and activist who has often been cited as the most iconic figure in modern architecture in post-independence India. He is best known for his sensitivity to the needs of the urban poor and for his use of traditional methods and materials.

Builder of the Nation

Correa studied at St Xavier's College, Mumbai and went on to specialise in architecture at the University of Michigan and Massachusetts Institute of Technology, USA. In 1958, he established his own Mumbai-based professional practice, Charles Correa Associates. In 1984, he founded the Urban Design Research Institute in Mumbai, which is dedicated to protecting the environment and improving urban communities.

During his lifetime, Correa designed close to 100 buildings in India alone and his work stands out for its sensitive design. Whether it was low-income housing, high-rise buildings in Mumbai or luxury condos in Goa, Correa respected local conditions and built practical structures that enhance the environment around them.

His work was heavily influenced by traditional Indian architecture in terms of design and use of local materials. This not only helped reduce expenses, but also provided work to local craftsmen. Correa's work is also known for his 'open-to-sky' concept that incorporated innovative methods of heating and cooling buildings by using pergolas, verandas, open courtyards and terraces. These structures bring with them light, circulation of air and plenty of shade.

Global Citizen

Correa's body of work includes some national and global landmarks like the Gandhi Smarak Sangrahalaya in Ahmedabad, Bharat Bhavan in Bhopal, Jawahar Kala Kendra in Jaipur, the Ismaili Centre in Toronto, Canada, Champalimaud Centre for the Unknown in Portugal, the Permanent Mission of India in New York, USA, the Handloom Pavilion in New Delhi and low-income sustainable tube houses in Ahmedabad.

During his lifetime, Correa designed close to 100 buildings in India alone and his work stands out for its sensitive design. Whether it was low-income housing, high-rise buildings in Mumbai or luxury condos in Goa, Correa respected local conditions and built practical structures that enhance the environment around them.

In the 1970s, Correa was appointed as the chief architect of Mumbai's satellite suburb, Navi Mumbai. Correa planned Navi Mumbai as a bazaar city with all the elements that are now considered as essential components of sustainable urbanisation. The project addressed issues such as affordability, mass transport, organised urban layouts and housing patterns that make the best use of space. Correa believed that cities are the nucleus for the country's economy and that unless land is well-designed with low-cost housing and amenities like schools and parks, slums and pavement dwellers cannot be wished away.

Awards Galore

During his lifetime, Correa was honoured with several prestigious awards. He was awarded the Padma Shri in 1972 and the Padma Vibhushan in 2006. He was also a recipient of the Aga Khan Award for Architecture in 1998 for his outstanding work for the Madhya Pradesh Legislative Assembly. In 2011, Correa was bestowed with Goa's highest civilian honour, the Gomant Vibhushan. In 2013, the Royal Institute of British Architects honoured him with a retrospective, hailing him as India's greatest architect.

CHANDRASEKHARA VENKATA RAMAN

7 November 1888 - 21 November 1970

Birthplace: Tiruchirappalli, Tamil Nadu

Claim to Fame: First Asian Nobel Prize winner in the field of science

'The essence of science is independent thinking, hard work, and not equipment. When I got my Nobel Prize, I had spent hardly ₹200 on my equipment.'

C V RAMAN

Physicist

Chandrasekhara Venkata Raman, popularly known as C V Raman, was a famous Indian physicist. He was raised in a large family and had seven siblings. Raman's father was a lecturer in mathematics and physics and was a great influence on young Raman. From a very early age, Raman would read physics books from his father's college library, and during vacations he would demonstrate experiments to his younger siblings.

In 1902, Raman entered Presidency College, Chennai and passed his bachelor's examination two years later, topping in both physics and English. In 1907, he earned his master's degree, obtaining the highest marks yet again. Raman's outstanding potential was recognised by many, which allowed him unlimited access to carry out experiments in his college laboratories. His earliest research in optics and acoustics – the two fields he dedicated his entire career to – were carried out when he was still a student.

Pursuit of Science

Despite his intent to pursue a career in science, Raman was persuaded to take up a civil service job. For ten years, he worked as a civil servant in the Indian Finance Department in Kolkata. In his free time, he carried out research on the physics of string instruments and drums. In addition to his research work, he gave public lectures in Kolkata on various scientific subjects. In 1917, Raman was appointed the first Palit Professor of Physics at the University of Calcutta and resigned from government service.

In 1930, Raman won the Nobel Prize in Physics for the discovery that when light travels through a transparent material, some of it gets deflected and changes in wavelength. This phenomenon is now called the Raman effect. His prize-winning work was inspired by observations he made on a sea voyage. He was the first Asian to receive a Nobel Prize in science and he was so confident of his work that he booked tickets to Sweden to receive the prize months before the winner was announced!

Raman also discovered that when light interacts with a molecule, it donates a small amount of energy to the molecule. As a result of this, the light changes colour and the molecule vibrates. The change of colour acts as a 'fingerprint' for the molecule. This study went into creating Raman spectroscopy, which is used in laboratories all over the world to identify molecules and analyse living cells and tissues to detect diseases such as cancer. His other work included studying the effects of x-rays on infrared vibrations in crystals exposed to light.

In 1930, Raman won the Nobel Prize in Physics for the discovery that when light travels through a transparent material, some of it gets deflected and changes in wavelength. This phenomenon is now called the Raman effect. His prize-winning work was inspired by observations he made on a sea voyage.

Professor to the Nation

In 1933, Raman became the first Indian director of the Indian Institute of Science in Bengaluru. In 1947, he became independent India's first National Professor. In 1948, Raman founded the Raman Research Institute in Bengaluru, where he served as the director until the end of his life. He also founded *Indian Journal of Physics*, of which he was the editor.

During his lifetime, Raman was honoured with a number of awards, including the Bharat Ratna, India's highest civilian honour, in 1954. He also received several honorary doctorates and memberships of scientific societies across the world. In 1924, he was elected as a fellow of the Royal Society, UK and in 1929, he was knighted by the British government in India.

DHIRAJLAL HIRACHAND AMBANI

28 December 1932 - 6 July 2002

Birthplace: Junagarh, Gujarat

Claim to Fame: Started one of India's largest conglomerates, Reliance Industries Limited

'Think big, think fast, think ahead. Ideas are no one's monopoly.'

DHIRUBHAI AMBANI

Businessman

Dhirajlal Hirachand Ambani, better known as Dhirubhai Ambani, was a renowned businessman who started one of India's largest conglomerates and one of the world's top companies, Reliance Industries Limited. Ambani remained a dominant figure in the textile, petroleum, power and infrastructure industries of India all his life.

Ambani was born to a schoolteacher father and a homemaker mother in a small village in the Junagarh district of Gujarat. He was raised with limited means along with his four siblings—Trilochanaben, Ramnikbhai, Jasuben and Natubhai. While growing up, Ambani had little interest in formal education but showed great skills in retailing and setting up small businesses to earn money and help his family. When he moved to Junagarh for his further studies, he actively participated in protests and became a patriotic rebel who supported the vision of independent India.

Being a business-minded person, Ambani always dreamt of a progressive India, where large industries would flourish. His social and political interests made him determined to do his bit for the country, and for himself. However, his father's failing health and his family's financial crisis forced Ambani to give up his education and interests and go to Aden, Yemen to find work.

New Learnings on Foreign Shores

When Ambani went to Aden, it was the one of the largest and busiest trading and oil bunkering ports in the world. The port was handling over 6,500 ships in a year, with goods landing from across the world and being distributed to faraway places. In Aden, Ambani started working as a clerk in the largest transcontinental trading firm in the region, A. Besse & Co. The firm was engaged in almost every branch of trading, from cargo booking and handling to shipping and wholesale merchandising. The firm dealt with various European, American, African and Asian companies and in all sorts of goods ranging from sugar, spices and textiles to machinery and petroleum products.

Ambani always dreamt of a progressive India, where large industries would flourish.

Working at A. Besse & Co. helped Ambani garner an insight into the trading business. He used this opportunity to learn about the various arms of trade. He also learnt about currency trading and money management. In fact, he was so proactive and ambitious that he even picked up the local language and became a fluent speaker. Soon, he began moonlighting at a Gujarati trading firm where he mastered accounting and drafting legal documents.

Building a New India

After nearly eight years, when most Indians in Aden were migrating to Britain for better opportunities, Ambani returned to India. Back in India, Ambani realised he had limited funds to start any purposeful business of his own. Instead, he got in touch with his Arabian contacts, offering to export spices, sugar and other commodities at very low prices. He chose to deal in bulk and as the large orders began coming in, Reliance Commercial Corporation was born. It became a huge success, but when Ambani realised that commodities would not take him very far, he decided to diversify into yarn.

Ambani borrowed heavily and set up his first textile mill in Naroda, Ahmedabad. His persuasiveness and sound marketing strategies helped the mill reach dazzling heights. His products reached right to the interiors of India and he equipped his factory with the best available technologies to raise production to meet growing demands. Once the company embarked on its successful journey, there was no looking back. Reliance went from being a ₹70 crore company in the mid-1970s to an exemplary ₹75,000 crore empire in the early 2000s.

Over the years, the company diversified into several other sectors such as energy, retail, telecommunication, logistics and information technology. By the time Ambani died in 2002, he had become a national hero. In 2016, he was honoured posthumously with the Padma Vibhushan, India's second highest civilian honour, for his contributions to trade and industry.

ELATTUVALAPIL SREEDHARAN

Born on: 12 June 1932

Birthplace: Palakkad, Kerala

Claim to Fame: Pivotal role in building the Konkan Railway and Delhi Metro

'The best way to motivate people is to set an example for them. I can't sit in an air-conditioned room and make others do all the work.'

E SREEDHARAN

Railway Engineer

Elattuvalapil Sreedharan, popularly known as the 'Metro Man', played a key role in building the Konkan Railway, which reduced the distance between Mumbai and Kochi by one third; and the Delhi Metro, which he delivered in three years, instead of the anticipated ten.

Sreedharan comes from a humble background. After having completed his civil engineering in Kakinada, Andhra Pradesh, he sought a job as a lecturer in civil engineering at the Government Polytechnic, Kozhikode. In 1953, he appeared for the Engineering Services Examination conducted by the Union Public Service Commission and soon after, he joined the Indian Engineering Services as a probationary assistant engineer in the Southern Railway in December 1954.

Surpassing Expectations

One of the biggest challenges Sreedharan faced during his tenure in the Southern Railway was that of rebuilding the damaged Pamban Bridge in Tamil Nadu after a cyclone had destroyed it. The railways had allotted six months for the repair work, but his boss wanted the work completed within three. Sreedharan managed to rebuild the bridge in forty-six days. This was one of the biggest stepping stones to his future career.

In 1970, Sreedharan was asked to plan, design and build the Kolkata Metro, the first metro in India. This was one of the largest infrastructure engineering projects in India at the time, which Sreedharan successfully completed in spite of many delays.

Sreedharan slowly grew through the ranks till he was elevated to the post of member engineering, Railway Board and ex-officio secretary to the government of India. When he retired from active duty in June 1990, the government appointed him chairman and managing director of the Konkan Railway on contract.

Sreedharan spearheaded the Konkan Railway project with a total tunnel length of 82 kilometres and ninety-three tunnels. The project involved tunnelling through 760 kilometres of soft soil and building 150 bridges. When the government was out of money for the project, he raised money through public bonds, becoming perhaps the first person in railway history to do so. Under his leadership, the work was completed in record time.

One of the biggest challenges Sreedharan faced during his tenure in the Southern Railway was that of rebuilding the damaged Pamban Bridge in Tamil Nadu after a cyclone had destroyed it. The railways had allotted six months for the repair work, but his boss wanted the work completed within three. Sreedharan managed to rebuild the bridge in forty-six days. This was one of the biggest stepping stones to his future career.

METRO MAN

Sreedharan was then brought in to head the Delhi Metro Rail Corporation (DMRC). Under his leadership, the DMRC regularly completed sections before target and is one of the few metro projects to run at a profit. In just over two decades, the Delhi Metro has changed the face of public transport in Delhi and the National Capital Region and its phenomenal success has brought Sreedharan many awards. After 2011, Sreedharan retired from the Delhi Metro and took on advisory roles in the Kochi Metro, Jaipur Metro, Lucknow Metro, Coimbatore Metro and proposed projects in Visakhapatnam and Vijayawada.

In 2001, Sreedharan was honoured with the Padma Shri, the fourth highest civilian honour in India. In 2003, Sreedharan was named one of Asia's Heroes by *Time Magazine*. In 2005, the government of France bestowed upon him the National Order of the Legion of Honour, the highest decoration in France. In 2008, he received the Padma Vibhushan, the second highest civilian honour in India, in recognition of his work with the Delhi Metro.

ELA RAMESH BHATT

Born on: 7 September 1933

Birthplace: Ahmedabad, Gujarat

Claim to Fame: Established SEWA, an NGO that serves the needs of poor, vulnerable women

*'There are risks in every action.
Every success has the seed of
some failure. But it doesn't matter.
It is how you go about it.
That is the real challenge.'*

ELA BHATT

Women's Rights Activist

In many Indian languages, 'sewa' means 'to serve someone'. SEWA is also an organisation that has served the needs of poor, vulnerable women for over forty-five years. SEWA is the vision of an extraordinary lady called Ela Ramesh Bhatt.

Bhatt was a bright student and did her early schooling and college from Surat. She went on to procure a law degree from Sir LA Shah Law College in Ahmedabad where she was also awarded a gold medal for her work on Hindu law. After completing her education, Bhatt briefly taught English at the SNDT University in Mumbai, but teaching was not a profession she enjoyed much.

After her stint at SNDT University, Bhatt returned to Ahmedabad where she joined the Textile Labour Association (TLA) in the legal department. In 1971, she had the opportunity to travel to Israel where she studied at the Afro-Asian Institute of Labour and Cooperatives in Tel Aviv for three months and received an international diploma in labour and cooperatives. In Israel, Bhatt noticed that every sector of Israeli labour was organised and the wives of workers were also union members. This inspired her to think of how she could put such a concept in place in Ahmedabad.

Of Service and Welfare

Bhatt was aware that many wives and daughters of textile workers worked as self-employed junk-smiths, garment makers, vegetable vendors and hawkers to supplement their family income. However, due to state laws, only industrially-employed women were protected and not self-employed ones. Bhatt also discovered that self-employed women were not even included in the 1971 census as workers! With the help of the president of TLA at the time, she began to organise the self-employed women into a union, which was established as SEWA with Bhatt as the general-secretary.

> *Bhatt also discovered that self-employed women were not even included in the 1971 census as workers!*

Founded as a trade union in 1972, SEWA works for the welfare of poor, self-employed women workers who form the bulk of the labour force in India. At the time in Ahmedabad, vegetables were distributed largely by women going from door to door, carrying the vegetables in small handcarts. Similarly, two-thirds of Ahmedabad received milk delivered by self-employed women who got up at dawn to feed and milk the cattle and prepare for the day's deliveries. Junk-smiths were another category of self-employed women who worked long hours, but still remained among the poorest. These were the women who were attracted to SEWA, the only organisation that had their interests at heart, and in only a few years the membership grew to over 5,000 women. SEWA soon expanded its activities to include a bank called SEWA Co-operative Bank for its members.

Fighting Poverty

A philanthropist at heart, Bhatt has done commendable work in the fields of international labour, women's development and micro-finance and has won many national and international awards. Bhatt is one of the founders of Women's World Banking and served as its chair from 1980 to 1998. She was also a trustee of the Rockefeller Foundation. Bhatt was awarded the Ramon Magsaysay Award for Community Leadership in 1977, the Right Livelihood Award in 1984, the Padma Shri in 1985 and the Padma Bhushan in 1986. She was also granted an honorary doctorate degree in humane letters by Harvard University, USA in June 2001.

More recently, she was chosen for the Niwano Peace Prize for 2010 for her contribution to the upliftment of poor women in India. At the ceremony in Tokyo, Japan, where she received her award, her acceptance speech spoke about women, work and peace. She talked about how respectable work will allow women to uplift themselves and their families from poverty and how women can then contribute to building peaceful communities.

HOMAI VYARAWALLA

9 December 1913 - 15 January 2012

Birthplace: Navsari, Gujarat

Claim to Fame: India's first woman photojournalist

'There are fifteen people taking a photograph at the same time; each has his own style. But there's only one who gets the right moment and the right angle.'

HOMAI VYARAWALLA

Photojournalist

Best known for documenting India's transition from a British colony to a newly independent nation, Homai Vyarawalla was born in a small Parsi town called Navsari in Gujarat. Her father was an actor in a travelling theatre group and she spent most of her childhood on the move. Eventually, the family settled in Mumbai where she attended the JJ School of Art.

While in college, she met Manekshaw Vyarawalla, a freelance photographer who introduced her to photography. Her first assignment at college was to photograph a picnic and her pictures were published in a local newspaper called *The Bombay Chronicle*. After that, she became a regular contributor to the paper as well as other publications including *The Illustrated Weekly of India*.

DEFINING IMAGES

Vyarawalla's photographs defined the modern woman of India. But when India got its independence, Indian women lost a lot of their freedoms. Women who dressed in modern clothes and had liberal views were looked down upon. The lives of Indian women became more restricted and women from aristocratic or upper class families were no longer allowed to get themselves photographed. As a result, Vyarawalla moved to taking political photographs.

After her marriage to Manekshaw, she settled in Delhi and joined the British Information Services as a news photographer. Many of her published images appeared under the pseudonym Dalda 13, derived from the license plate of her first car, DLD 13.

Vyarawalla rose to the top of a male-dominated field and on this she is known to have said, 'Somehow it never occurred to me that I was doing something unusual or that I was the only woman in a male-dominated profession at that time. I think I was casual in my dressing and unobtrusive in my demeanour, so this may have made people around me feel at ease. I was always given due credit for my work and was respected just as any other competent person in the field. At school, I was the only girl in my matriculation class. So I was used to being in the company of boys.'

The lives of Indian women became more restricted and women from aristocratic or upper class families were no longer allowed to get themselves photographed. As a result, Vyarawalla moved to taking political photographs.

Chronicling India's History

Through her forty-year career, Vyarawalla photographed many iconic events including the departure of Lord Mountbatten, the first raising of independent India's flag, Mahatma Gandhi's cremation and Dalai Lama's arrival in India. In 1969, when her husband passed away, Vyarawalla moved to Rajasthan and later, Gujarat, and gave up working as a professional photographer. Her last picture, of Indira Gandhi, was taken in 1970.

In 2010, Vyarawalla received the first National Photo Award for Lifetime Achievement. She was awarded the Padma Vibhushan in 2011 and the Lifetime Achievement Award by the information and broadcasting ministry in the same year. Before her death in 2012, Vyarawalla donated all her works to the Alkazi Foundation.

HOMI JEHANGIR BHABHA

30 October 1909 - 24 January 1966

Birthplace: Mumbai, Maharashtra

Claim to Fame: 'Father of the Indian Nuclear Programme'

'My success will not depend on what A or B thinks of me. My success will be what I make of my work.'

HOMI BHABHA

Nuclear Physicist

Homi Jehangir Bhabha was a nuclear physicist who played a key role in the development of India's nuclear energy programme. He made important contributions to the study of quantum theory and cosmic radiation and went on to lead the country's nuclear establishments for the first two decades after independence. He was thus regarded as the 'Father of the Indian Nuclear Programme'.

Bhabha was born into a wealthy and extremely influential Parsi family in Mumbai. His father was a lawyer and his mother was the granddaughter of Dinshaw Petit, a well-known philanthropist. He was also related to the eminent Indian businessman, Dorabji Tata. Given his aristocratic background, Bhabha was surrounded by prominent individuals and had access to books, music, art and travel.

Education as a Foundation

At the age of fifteen, Bhabha enrolled at Elphinstone College and later studied at the Royal Institute of Science in Mumbai. Dorabji Tata wanted him to join his Tata Steel Company so Bhabha began studying mechanical engineering at University of Cambridge, UK. However, he soon developed a growing interest in theoretical physics and mathematics under the influence of English physicist Paul Dirac. In 1930, he passed the Mechanical Engineering Tripos with a first class. Bhabha remained at the university with his family's approval and began studying and conducting research in theoretical physics. In 1934, he received his doctorate degree in nuclear physics.

Securing India's Future

Bhabha took the post of reader at the Indian Institute of Science, Bengaluru at the behest of Nobel Prize-winning physicist C V Raman. He was soon promoted and held the post of professor at the institute's cosmic ray research unit. With time, Bhabha realised that the development of nuclear energy was crucial for the future industrial growth of the country. He immediately sent a proposal to the Tata Trust on establishing a school of research in fundamental physics. The trustees approved and in 1945, the Tata Institute of Fundamental Research was established in Mumbai. Later, in 1954, he helped the Indian government set up the Atomic Energy Establishment in Trombay, Mumbai to conduct large-scale research in physics, chemistry, electronics and mathematics.

With time, Bhabha realised that the development of nuclear energy was crucial for the future industrial growth of the country.

Soon after India's independence, Bhabha sent a note to the then Prime Minister Jawaharlal Nehru, proposing the formation of the Atomic Energy Commission that would direct the development of India's nuclear energy programme for peaceful purposes. The commission was successfully established in 1948 and Bhabha served as its first chairperson. Bhabha developed a strategy of extracting power from thorium, rather than uranium, as thorium was present in abundance in the country. This thorium-focused strategy was in marked contrast to that of all other countries in the world and resulted in the development of India's three-stage nuclear power programme.

Advocate of Peace

Bhabha advocated the peaceful use of nuclear energy and was against using it for war. He voiced his concerns over the misuse of nuclear power at many international platforms and represented India at several international atomic energy forums. He was also the president of the first United Nations Conference on the Peaceful Uses of Atomic Energy, held in Geneva, Switzerland in 1955.

Bhabha received the Padma Bhushan for his invaluable contributions to science and engineering in 1954. He died an untimely death in an air crash in 1966 and after his death, the Atomic Energy Establishment was renamed as the Bhabha Atomic Research Centre in his honour.

JAYANT VISHNU NARLIKAR

Born on: 19 July 1938

Birthplace: Kolhapur, Maharashtra

Claim to Fame: Conducted pioneering research work in astronomy and cosmology

'Whatever you do, give your best to it.'

JAYANT NARLIKAR

Astrophysicist

Jayant Vishnu Narlikar is an astrophysicist who is known for his pioneering research in astronomy and cosmology, especially in championing models alternative to the popular big bang model.

Narlikar was born into a family of scholars in Kolhapur, Maharashtra. His father was the head of the mathematics department at the Banaras Hindu University in Uttar Pradesh while his mother was a scholar of Sanskrit.

Narlikar was an exceptionally talented student who always topped school and college examinations. He completed his bachelor's degree in science from Banaras Hindu University, where he topped his class. He then began his higher studies in mathematics at University of Cambridge, UK. He obtained his master's degree in astronomy and astrophysics and received his PhD under the guidance of famous British astronomer and astrophysicist, Fred Hoyle.

Challenging Ideas

Narlikar's PhD thesis included research on principles of gravitation and gravitational pull between different celestial bodies and the formation of the universe. Along with Hoyle, he developed the Hoyle-Narlikar theory, which presented a different view on the big bang theory to explain how the solar system was formed.

While still a student at Cambridge, he won the Tyson Medal for astronomy in 1960 and the Smith's Prize in 1962. At the age of twenty-two, Narlikar became a member of the Royal Astronomical Society and was appointed as a fellow at the Kings College in Cambridge University. He was also a founding staff member of the Institute of Theoretical Astronomy in Cambridge, which was created by Hoyle.

> *Narlikar's PhD thesis included research on principles of gravitation and gravitational pull between different celestial bodies and the formation of the universe.*

Narlikar lived abroad for fifteen years before returning to India. Upon his return, he worked as a professor at the Tata Institute of Fundamental Research in Mumbai. Under his guidance, the Theoretical Astrophysics Group at the institute developed into a leading learning centre for the subject. After a few years, the Indian University Grants Commission set up the Inter-University Centre for Astronomy and Astrophysics in Pune and Narlikar became its founder-director. Under his guidance and leadership, the centre soon became an institute of international acclaim.

Science Advocate

Apart from his scientific research, Narlikar has worked towards popularising science and is known for his science writing, radio shows and television programmes. Narlikar has also served as the chairperson of the Advisory Group for Textbooks in Science and Mathematics, the committee responsible for developing textbooks on science and mathematics.

For his pioneering work, Narlikar has received several national and international awards and honorary doctorates including the prestigious Padma Bhushan in 1965 and the Padma Vibhushan in 2004. He has also been honoured with the Kalinga Prize by UNESCO in 1996 for popularising science and the Sahitya Akademi Award in 2014 for his autobiography in Marathi.

JEHANGIR RATANJI DADABHOY TATA

29 July 1904 - 29 November 1993

Birthplace: Paris, France

Claim to Fame: Entrepreneur, businessman, chairman of the Tata Group and 'Father of Indian Civil Aviation'

'Never start with diffidence,
always start with confidence.'

J R D TATA

Industrialist

Jehangir Ratanji Dadabhoy Tata, better known as J R D Tata, was a French-born Indian aviator, businessman and pioneering industrialist. He was born into a very wealthy family that established one of the country's largest business conglomerates, the Tata Group.

Tata grew up imbibing two cultures—one from his French mother and the other from his Parsi father. He spent most of his childhood in France and studied in various countries including Japan, England and India. As a young man, he met French aviation pioneer Louis Blériot, an encounter that kindled his lifelong passion for flying. While in France, Tata was commissioned into the French Army as part of the country's law requiring one-year compulsory service. After completing his service, Tata moved to London to pursue further education, but he was compelled to return to India and assume his role in the family business.

Setting Flight

In India, Tata began working as an apprentice in Tata Sons, the Tata Group's flagship company. At the age of twenty-five, he renounced his French citizenship and became an Indian citizen. Tata's passion for aviation led him to become the first Indian to obtain a pilot's license issued in India. He turned his passion into a business when in 1932, he established India's first commercial airlines, Tata Airlines, which was later acquired by the Indian government and re-branded as Air India. The airline went on to become one the largest in the Indian subcontinent. In 1953, the government of India appointed Tata as the chairman of Air India and a director on the board of Indian Airlines—a post he retained for twenty-five years. For his exceptional achievements in aviation, he came to be known as the 'Father of Indian Civil Aviation'.

At thirty-four, Tata took charge as the chairman of Tata Sons and became the youngest member of the board. He served the position for over fifty years, during which time the

Tata Group expanded into several new horizons and became one of India's most trusted brands. Under his leadership, the company's assets climbed from ₹62 crore in 1939 to more than ₹10,000 crore in 1990. When Tata began working, the Tata Group had fourteen enterprises. Today, the company is a conglomerate of over 100 enterprises.

When Tata began working, the Tata Group had fourteen enterprises. Today, the company is a conglomerate of over 100 enterprises.

BUILDER OF INSTITUTIONS

In 1936, Tata founded the Tata Institute of Social Sciences in Mumbai. Under his guidance, the Tata Trust also established Asia's first cancer hospital, the Tata Memorial Hospital, in Mumbai in 1941. In 1945, Tata founded Tata Motors, a locomotive manufacturing company that dominated the Indian market for years. He also founded several other enterprises and institutions including Tata Consultancy Services, Titan Industries, Tata Salt, Voltas, Tata Institute of Fundamental Research, National Centre for Performing Arts and many more.

Tata was very concerned with the welfare of his workers. So, in 1956, Tata initiated a programme to provide them with good working conditions, which included an eight-hour working day, free medical aid and accident compensation schemes, provident fund and several other benefits. These were later adopted by the government as statutory requirements in India.

Over the years, Tata received numerous awards for his work. He was conferred with the honorary rank of group captain by the Indian Air Force in 1948. He was then promoted to the rank of air commodore and later to the rank of air vice marshal in 1974. He won the Daniel Guggenheim Medal for aviation in 1988 and the United Nations Population Award in 1992 for initiating and successfully implementing the family planning movement in India. He also became a recipient of the National Order of the Legion of Honour, the highest decoration in France for military and civil merits, in 1983. He was awarded the Padma Vibhushan in 1957 as well as India's highest civilian honour, the Bharat Ratna, in 1992 for his pioneering contributions to Indian industry and society.

KAILASH SATYARTHI

Born on: 11 January 1954

Birthplace: Vidisha, Madhya Pradesh

Claim to Fame: Nobel Prize-winning child rights activist

'Educating children is the key to sound, sustainable economic development in any nation.'

KAILASH SATYARTHI

Child Rights Activist

Born Kailash Sharma, Kailash Satyarthi has been actively involved in the movement against child labour in India since the 1980s. His organisation, Bachpan Bachao Andolan, has been responsible for freeing over 87,000 child slaves from numerous industries.

Satyarthi was born to a police constable father and an uneducated, idealistic homemaker mother. He first learnt to read Urdu from a religious teacher at a mosque near his home as a four-year-old and subsequently learnt Hindi and English in school. Even as a child, Satyarthi was well aware of discrimination. When he noticed a cobbler's son outside the school, he immediately asked his teacher why the boy was not attending school with them. When he didn't get a suitable answer from his teacher, he mustered enough courage to ask the cobbler the same question. The cobbler's answer, which put the blame on caste differences, made a big impact on Satyarthi. This was his first lesson in life—that discrimination is inbuilt in society.

SAVING CHILDHOODS

Satyarthi and his friends soon started donating books to children who could not afford new books and set up a small library for them. Satyarthi went on to study electrical engineering but gave it all up, including his job as a teacher, to start Bachpan Bachao Andolan in 1980. This was the first people's movement for social justice, equity, education and peace for all children in India. The organisation saves children from child labour, trafficking and other exploitative situations. After rescuing the children, Bachpan Bachao Andolan helps them with rehabilitation and education.

Satyarthi also published a fortnightly called *Sangharsh Jaari Rahega*, which focused primarily on the work done by people like him in an attempt to defend human rights.

In 1994, Satyarthi established Rugmark, now known as GoodWeave International, an organisation which monitors and provides certification of rugs manufactured by the rug industry in South Asia, certifying that their product is made without the use of child labour.

Satyarthi went on to study electrical engineering but gave it all up, including his job as a teacher, to start Bachpan Bachao Andolan in 1980.

Satyarthi organised the Global March Against Child Labour across 103 countries in 1998. With 7.2 million people and 20,000 civil society organisations participating, this was the largest people's campaign on child labour. As a global voice against child labour, he also works very closely with the international advocacy body, the International Center on Child Labour and Education, a worldwide coalition of NGOs, teachers and trade unionists.

More recently, Satyarthi established the Kailash Satyarthi Children's Foundation (KSCF), an organisation that engages with law enforcement agencies by training and sensitising them about national and international laws related to children. Satyarthi is also responsible for organising Bal Mitra Gram, a programme that creates child-friendly villages, where all children are enrolled in school. Launched in 2011, the programme has been adopted by over 350 villages till date.

Global Recognition

In 2014, Satyarthi was awarded the Nobel Peace Prize jointly with Malala Yousafzai for their struggle against the suppression of children and young people and for the right of all children to education. Satyarthi dedicated the entire prize sum to the advancement of the rights of children. On 7 January 2015, he gave his Nobel medal to the president of India, dedicating it to his motherland and its great people. The medal is now displayed at the Rashtrapati Bhawan Museum in New Delhi.

Satyarthi has been awarded many human rights awards and honours apart from the Nobel Peace Prize. His latest award is the Santokhba Humanitarian Award, which he received in 2018.

MAHASWETA DEVI

14 January 1926 - 28 July 2016

Birthplace: Dhaka, Bangladesh

Claim to Fame: Fiction writer and socio-political activist

*'Time was the arch fugitive,
always on the run.'*

MAHASWETA DEVI

Author and Activist

Mahasweta Devi was born in Dhaka, which was then a part of the Bengal Presidency. When India got its freedom, her family moved to West Bengal. She came from a very literate family; her parents were writers and her father was one of the most influential voices in Bengali literature.

Devi completed her pre-primary and primary education in Dhaka and high school in West Bengal. She also attended Santiniketan and Visva Bharti University before completing her master's degree in English from the University of Calcutta.

During the Bengal famine from 1942 to 1944, Devi volunteered to provide relief to the victims. She distributed food, helped people on the streets and carried the living to relief centres. During this time, she held various jobs, right from working in a post office and selling soaps and dye powder to supplying monkeys for research to the US and writing letters in English for illiterate people.

MOTHER OF THE SABARS

In 1964, Devi began teaching college students. During this period, she also worked as a journalist and creative writer. It was at this time that she met and started working with the Lodha and Sabar tribes of West Bengal. Her time spent with these tribes soon began seeping into her literary work, which began to depict the brutal oppression of tribal people by powerful upper-caste landlords, money-lenders and government officials. She actively opposed the acquisition of farmers' land to create industries and edited a tribal magazine called *Bartika*, which took her thoughts and those of the tribal people to the rest of the country. Her work in support of the Sabar tribe earned her the title, 'Mother of the Sabars'.

LITERARY FLAIR

Though Devi started writing at the age of thirteen, she only got recognised after her first book was published in 1956, by which time she was thirty years old. The book, titled *The Queen of Jhansi*, is a reconstruction of the life of Rani Lakshmi Bai based on extensive research using historical documents, folk tales, poetry and oral tradition. To complete this work, Devi travelled to villages where the tradition of oral story-telling was still alive.

During the Bengal famine from 1942 to 1944, Devi volunteered to provide relief to the victims. She distributed food, helped people on the streets and carried the living to relief centres. During this time, she held various jobs, right from working in a post office and selling soaps and dye powder to supplying monkeys for research to the US and writing letters in English for illiterate people.

During her lifetime, she authored more than 100 novels and twenty collections of short stories, some of which have also been adapted into screenplays for Bollywood movies. Devi's stories are extremely powerful and revolve around real-life situations and people. This has made her one of the best-known and most frequently translated Indian female authors.

Devi won many awards including the Sahitya Akademi Award in 1979, the Padma Shri in 1986, the Jnanpith Award in 1996 and the Padma Vibhushan in 2006. The Padma Shri was awarded to her for her work with the tribal groups of the Purulia and Medinipur districts of West Bengal. She also won the Ramon Magsaysay Award for Community Leadership in 1997 and was shortlisted for the Man Booker Prize in 2009.

MAQBOOL FIDA HUSAIN

17 September 1915 - 9 June 2011

Birthplace: Pandharpur, Maharashtra

Claim to Fame: Modern Indian painter, also known as the 'Picasso of India'

'You must have the courage to break out of your own image.'

M F HUSAIN

Artist

Maqbool Fida Husain, better known as M F Husain, was known for his bold, brightly coloured narrative paintings. His art was inspired by Cubism, a visual art style from the early twentieth century that was created in Paris, France by Pablo Picasso and Georges Braque.

Husain was born in the small town of Pandharpur in Maharashtra. He studied in Indore and discovered his artistic side while learning calligraphy at a madrassa in Baroda. He then went on to study art at the JJ School of Arts in Mumbai and began his career painting Bollywood hoardings using his characteristic freehand drawings. He also practised the Kufic style of Arabic calligraphy with its distinct geometric forms.

ART, FILMS AND MORE

Husain held his first serious exhibition in 1947 at the Bombay Art Society. This exhibition and India's independence were two major turning points in his career. He soon started gaining recognition for his work and also became acquainted with other like-minded artists like F N Souza and Tyeb Mehta, with whom he formed the Bombay Progressive Artists' Group.

While painting was his true love, Husain had to make furniture and toys to earn a living. He would then return to painting and work with a blend of folk, tribal, religious and mythological forms. He started depicting icons of Indian culture, characters from epics like the *Mahabharata* and people like Mahatma Gandhi and Saint Teresa in his work. He was also known for his paintings of free-spirited horses.

During the early 1950s, Husain went to Europe for the first time. He did a barefoot grand tour and met other painters like Picasso, Matisse and Paul Klee. He also held his first solo exhibition in Zurich, Switzerland at this time.

In the following decade, he ventured into film-making. His first film, *Through the Eyes of a Painter* was screened at the Berlin International Film Festival in Germany where it received the Golden Bear Award in 1967. He also received the National Film Award for Best Experimental Film for this movie. In 1971, he was a special invitee at the Sao Paulo Biennial in Brazil, which was also attended by Picasso.

While painting was his true love, Husain had to make furniture and toys to earn a living. He would then return to painting and work with a blend of folk, tribal, religious and mythological forms.

In the 1970s and 80s, Husain painted some of his most well-known works including *Vishwamitra* and *Passage Through Human Space*, a series of forty-five watercolours. However, he was accused of hurting religious sentiments when he portrayed Hindu deities in unconventional ways. After that, he went back to movies and directed three films, one of which was *Meenaxi: A Tale of Three Cities*, which was screened in the Marché du Film section of the 2004 Cannes Film Festival in France.

Making Home Away from Home

In 2008, Husain was commissioned to create ninety-nine pieces for the Museum of Islamic Art in Doha, Qatar. By 2010, he had become a citizen of Qatar and spent his time between there and England. Due to his controversial work, he was no longer welcome in India. During his stay in Qatar, he was commissioned by Qatar's first lady, Sheikha Mozah Bint Nasser Al Missned, to create two paintings depicting the history of Arab civilisation and the history of Indian civilisation. However, this work was left incomplete as he passed away in London in 2011.

The government of India honoured Husain with the Padma Shri in 1966, the Padma Bhushan in 1973 and the Padma Vibhushan in 1991 and appointed him to a term in the Rajya Sabha in recognition of his contribution to art. Husain was also part of a list of 500 most influential Muslims in the world, released by the Jordanian Royal Islamic Strategic Studies Centre. His artworks are displayed in several museums across the world.

MOKSHAGUNDAM VISVESVARAYA

15 September 1861 - 12 April 1962

Birthplace: Chikkaballapur, Karnataka

Claim to Fame: Eminent engineer and dam builder

'Remember, your work may be only to sweep a railway crossing, but it is your duty to keep it so clean that no other crossing in the world is as clean as yours.'

M VISVESVARAYA

Civil Engineer

Mokshagundam Visvesvaraya, better known as M Visvesvaraya, is regarded as India's most prolific civil engineer and dam builder. A scholar, statesman, politician and one of the most influential engineers of his time, he believed in simple living and the power of knowledge. To honour his immense contribution to society, Engineer's Day is celebrated annually in India on his birthday, 15th September.

Visvesvaraya was born in Muddenahalli village in south Karnataka's Chikkaballapur district. His father, who was a Sanskrit scholar, worked hard to provide his son with quality education. But his father died when he was only fifteen years old. After this, the family plunged into poverty and Visvesvaraya started tutoring children to pay for his education.

Visvesvaraya completed his primary education from his village and moved to Bengaluru for higher studies. After winning a scholarship from the Mysore government, he joined the College of Engineering in Pune, where he topped his class.

Rising through the Ranks

Soon after his graduation, Visvesvaraya found a job as an assistant engineer at the Public Works Department of Mumbai and worked across Khandesh, Nashik and Pune. He later joined the Indian Irrigation Commission and helped implement a complex irrigation system in the Deccan area. He successfully devised a method of supplying water from the Sindhu River to a small town called Sukkur. His work earned him popularity and the government of India sent him to Aden in Yemen to study water supply and drainage systems.

Visvesvaraya quickly moved up the ranks and was eventually appointed as the chief engineer of the princely state of Mysore. From 1912 to 1919, he also served as the diwan of Mysore State. During this time, he worked relentlessly for the overall development of the state. He charted out the plan for road construction between Tirumala and Tirupati and set up the Kannada Parishat for the upliftment of the Kannada language. He also laid the foundation of Jayanagar, a planned neighbourhood in Bengaluru, which was regarded as one of the best and largest planned layouts in Asia. He is thus known as the 'Father of the Modern Mysore State'.

> *Over the years, he helped establish several industries including the Sandal Oil and Soap Factory, the Chrome Tanning Factory and Bhadravathi Iron and Steel Works. Visvesvaraya also helped in building the Government Engineering College in Bengaluru, one of the first engineering institutes in India.*

Harnessing Water Resources

As an engineer, Visvesvaraya implemented many dam projects and is known the world over for his contribution to harnessing water resources. He was responsible for building and consolidating major dams across the country, including the Krishna Raja Sagar Dam in Mysuru. He is also credited with the development of the block system, which prevents the wasteful flow of water in dams. Additionally, Visvesvaraya served as a consulting engineer for a flood protection system for the city of Hyderabad, which was reeling under the threat of floods.

Over the years, he helped establish several industries including the Government Sandalwood Oil Factory, the Government Soap Factory, the Chrome Tanning Factory and Bhadravathi Iron and Steel Works. Visvesvaraya also helped in building the Government Engineering College in Bengaluru, one of the first engineering institutes in India. It was later renamed as the Visvesvaraya College of Engineering in his honour.

In 1915, Visvesvaraya was awarded British knighthood by King George V for his outstanding contributions to society. In 1955, he was awarded India's highest honour, the Bharat Ratna. He also received several honorary doctorate degrees from universities in India.

MADURAI SHANMUKHAVADIVU SUBBULAKSHMI

16 September 1916 - 11 December 2004

Birthplace: Madurai, Tamil Nadu

Claim to Fame: Exponent of Carnatic music

'Music is an ocean and I am a student. For a vocalist, voice practice is important. It has been my habit to learn the meaning of the songs I have to sing and the correct pronunciation of each word.'

M S SUBBULAKSHMI

Musician

Madurai Shanmukhavadivu Subbulakshmi or M S Subbulakshmi's name is synonymous with the world of Carnatic music. Subbulakshmi was born into a community of devadasis, women who dedicate their lives to the worship and service of a Hindu deity or temple. She was surrounded by music and her first teachers were her mother, who played the veena, and her grandmother, who played the violin. Music was literally in her genes and she often practised with her mother and grandmother before she got formal training in Carnatic and Hindustani music.

A Voice That Broke Barriers

Subbulakshmi's first recording was released when she was ten years old and she gave her first public performance at the age of eleven, in the 100-pillar hall inside the Rockfort Temple in Tiruchirappalli. By the time she was seventeen, Subbulakshmi was performing on her own, including major concerts at the Madras Music Academy. Carnatic music concerts were a domain traditionally reserved for men, but her melodious voice broke all barriers, earning her the title, 'Nightingale of Carnatic Music'.

By the time she was in her late teens, Subbulakshmi had to move to Chennai. This is where she met her future husband, Kalki Sadasivam, who introduced her to the world of cinema. She made her Tamil film debut at the age of twenty-two and acted in a few movies. Her role in a film called *Meera* catapulted her to fame. Around this time, she also performed for the likes of Mahatma Gandhi's wife Kasturba Gandhi, Jawaharlal Nehru and others. She soon started performing a vast variety of devotional musical forms in different languages including Tamil, Kannada, Sanskrit, Punjabi, Hindi, Malayalam, Telugu, Bengali, Gujarati and Marathi.

Over the years, Subbulakshmi became a cultural ambassador for India, performing at various prestigious venues across the world. In 1963, she participated in the Edinburgh International Festival in Scotland. In 1966, she performed at Carnegie Hall and later at the United Nations General Assembly in New York City, USA. In 1982, she sang at the Royal Albert Hall in London, UK. In India, she performed at the annual Thyagaraja Festival and Tirumala Tirupati Devasthanams.

Subbulakshmi's first recording was released when she was ten years old and she gave her first public performance at the age of eleven, in the 100-pillar hall inside the Rockfort Temple in Tiruchirappalli. By the time she was seventeen, Subbulakshmi was performing on her own, including major concerts at the Madras Music Academy.

Of Fame and Recognition

Apart from music, Subbulakshmi was known for her charity work; she would often give all the royalties she earned from her music to charity organisations. Subbulakshmi also won many awards. She was awarded the Padma Bhushan in 1954, the Sangeet Natak Akademi Award in 1956, the Sangeetha Kalanidhi in 1968, the Padma Vibhushan in 1975, the Kalidas Samman in 1988 and the Indira Gandhi Award for National Integration in 1990.

Subbulakshmi is the only Indian musician to be awarded the Ramon Magsaysay Award for Community Leadership, which she received in 1974, and the Bharat Ratna, India's highest civilian honour, which she received in 1998. She was also honoured as the court-singer of Tirumala Tirupati Devasthanams and the Tirupati Urban Development Authority installed a bronze statue of her at the Poornakumbham Circle in Tirupati. The famous Kancheepuram saree shade known as M S Blue has been named after her and the United Nations also issued a stamp to mark her birth centenary.

MANKOMBU SAMBASIVAN SWAMINATHAN

Born on: 7 August 1925

Birthplace: Kumbakonam, Tamil Nadu

Claim to Fame: 'Father of the Green Revolution in India' and 'Father of Economic Ecology'

'If agriculture goes wrong, nothing else will have a chance to go right in our country.'

M S SWAMINATHAN

Geneticist

Mankombu Sambasivan Swaminathan, better known as M S Swaminathan, is a renowned Indian geneticist who orchestrated the success of the Green Revolution programme in India. He is known for his leadership and success in introducing and further developing high-yielding varieties of wheat. His contributions have made an indelible mark on food production in India and other developing countries around the world.

Swaminathan's family was among the most important in their village and he was highly influenced by his surgeon and social reformer father. However, his father died when Swaminathan was just eleven years old. Thereafter, he was raised by his uncle, who was a radiologist.

Passion for Genetics

After graduating in zoology, Swaminathan obtained a second bachelor's degree in agricultural science from the Madras Agricultural College. Swaminathan then joined the Indian Agricultural Research Institute (IARI) in New Delhi and pursued his post-graduation in genetics and plant breeding. His decision to take up the study of genetics was influenced by the great Bengal famine of 1943 during which food shortages resulted in countless deaths. Getting rid of hunger and poverty became Swaminathan's ultimate goal.

In 1949, he received a UNESCO Fellowship and went to Wageningen Agricultural University in the Netherlands. There he continued his research on potato genetics and succeeded in standardising procedures for transferring genes from a wide range of wild species of potato to cultivated potatoes. A few years later, he moved to the Plant Breeding Institute of the University of Cambridge School of Agriculture, UK and earned his PhD. He then accepted a post-doctoral research associateship at the University of Wisconsin, USA to help set up a United States Department of Agriculture Potato

Research Station. Despite all the facilities that were available to him during this stint, Swaminathan declined the offer of a full-time faculty role and returned to India.

> *His decision to take up the study of genetics was influenced by the great Bengal famine of 1943 during which food shortages resulted in countless deaths. Getting rid of hunger and poverty became Swaminathan's ultimate goal.*

Seeding India's Food Security

In India, Swaminathan re-joined IARI as a teacher and research administrator and went on to become the institution's director. Over the years, his work included solving a range of problems in plant breeding, agricultural research and development and conservation of natural resources. This helped India achieve a substantial increase in the production of wheat and rice and this achievement was termed as the Green Revolution.

Swaminathan has also been called the 'Father of Economic Ecology' by the United Nations Environment Programme for his contribution towards economic growth via farmlands. He led India to sustainable development through environmentally sustainable agriculture, sustainable food security and the preservation of biodiversity.

Through the course of his career, Swaminathan has been honoured with several national and international awards for his contributions to agriculture and biodiversity preservation. He is a recipient of the prestigious Ramon Magsaysay Award for Community Leadership in 1971, the Albert Einstein World Science Award in 1986, the UNESCO Mahatma Gandhi Prize in 2000, the Lal Bahadur Shastri National Award in 2007 as well as the Padma Shri in 1967, the Padma Bhushan in 1972 and the Padma Vibushan in 1989. He has received more than seventy honorary PhD degrees from universities across the world and in 1999, he was named by *Time Magazine* as one of the twenty most influential Asians of the twentieth century. In fact, he was one of only three Indians on the list; the other two were Rabindranath Tagore and Mahatma Gandhi.

MUNSHI PREMCHAND

31 July 1880 - 8 October 1936

Birthplace: Varanasi, Uttar Pradesh

Claim to Fame: Novelist and author

‘Trees bear fruits only to be eaten by others; the fields grow grains, but they are consumed by the world. Cows give milk, but she doesn’t drink it herself–that is left to others. Clouds send rain only to quench the parched earth. In such giving, there is little space for selfishness.’

MUNSHI PREMCHAND

Author

Munshi Premchand is considered to be one of the greatest Hindi writers of the twentieth century. A teacher by profession, he began his literary career as a freelancer in Urdu but soon started writing short stories and novels in Hindi. His stories carried important social messages, often speaking about the inhumane treatment meted out to girls and women.

Premchand was born as Dhanpat Rai Srivastav in Lamhi, Varanasi. His name Dhanpat means 'master of wealth'. His father Ajaib Rai worked at the post office and his mother Anandi Devi was a homemaker. He received his early education at a madrassa where he learnt Urdu and Persian. He lost his mother at an early age and sought solace in books. In fact, he also took up a job as a bookseller so he could read more.

To support his family, he started tutoring children. When his father died in 1897, he had to discontinue his education to look after his siblings and step-siblings. Around the same time, he was asked to join the Government District School in Bahraich as an assistant teacher. This was also the time when he started writing fiction and initially wrote under the pen name Nawab Rai.

Becoming Premchand

In 1905, Premchand shifted to Kanpur and met Daya Narain Nigam, the editor of a magazine called *Zamana*. A patriot at heart, Premchand wrote many stories in Urdu encouraging people to participate in the struggle for freedom. When the British got their hands on these articles, which were published in the form of a short story collection titled *Soz-e-Watan*, he was forced to change his pen name to Premchand in order to escape imprisonment.

By the mid-1910s, he became a prominent writer in Urdu and then in Hindi. His first major Hindi novel, *Seva Sadan* was published in 1919. In 1921, Premchand gave up his government job to join Mahatma Gandhi's Non-cooperation Movement.

Premchand soon moved to Varanasi to continue work on his literary career. In 1923, he established a publishing house called Saraswati Press. Over the next decade, he started a political weekly called *Hans*, taught at the Marwari College in Kanpur, worked as an editor of *Maryada* magazine in Varanasi and served as a headmaster at Kashi Vidyapeeth. In 1931, he moved to Mumbai and worked as a scriptwriter for Ajanta Cinetone, a production house. However, this life didn't suit him and he moved back to his hometown.

A patriot at heart, Premchand wrote many stories in Urdu encouraging people to participate in the struggle for freedom. When the British got their hands on these articles, which were published in the form of a short story collection titled Soz-e-Watan, he was forced to change his pen name to Premchand in order to escape imprisonment.

Literary Legacy

Premchand's stories are simple and depict honest human emotions. His works have been translated into many languages including English, Russian and Chinese. Many of his works have also been made into movies and television serials. Satyajit Ray made two movies based on Premchand's works, *Sadgati* and *Shatranj Ke Khiladi*. Premchand died whilst writing *Mangalsutra*, a novel that remains unfinished.

In 1936, a few months before his death, Premchand was elected as the first president of the Progressive Writers' Association in Lucknow. The Sahitya Akademi, India's national academy of letters, established the Premchand Fellowships in his honour in 2005. They are given to persons of eminence in the field of culture from South Asian Association for Regional Cooperation (SAARC) countries.

NAGAVARA RAMARAO NARAYANA MURTHY

Born on: 20 August 1946

Birthplace: Shidlaghatta, Karnataka

Claim to Fame: Established Infosys, a multinational information technology company

'Leaders should lead by example in aspiration, optimism, hard work, monetary and other sacrifices.'

N R NARAYANA MURTHY

Entrepreneur

Nagavara Ramarao Narayana Murthy, better known as N R Narayana Murthy, is the co-founder of India's second-largest information technology company, Infosys Limited. He played a prominent role in nurturing the company, building it from scratch along with six other founding members.

Murthy was born and raised in a middle-class family in Karnataka. After attending a government school, he appeared for the entrance test for the Indian Institute of Technology (IIT) and cleared it with a high rank and a scholarship. However, the scholarship did not cover his educational expenses and his father could not afford to pay the fees. His father advised him to join a local engineering college, the National Institute of Engineering in Mysuru, and he graduated in 1967 with a degree in electrical engineering. He then went on to get his master's degree from IIT Kanpur.

Early Learnings

In the 1970s, Murthy moved to France where he worked in a company called SESA for three years. While working with SESA, he excelled in designing software for air-freight management at the Charles De Gaulle airport in Paris. This experience inspired him to return to India to start his own company.

In India, Murthy started his career as a chief systems programmer at the Indian Institute of Management (IIM), Ahmedabad. He considers working here to be one of the best learning experiences of his professional life. Later, he started a software consulting firm called Softronics in Pune, which failed within a year and a half. He eventually joined Patni Computer Systems as a general manager and worked there for several years.

Small Beginnings, Big Ambitions

In 1981, Murthy decided to become an entrepreneur again. Along with six other software professionals, he founded a company called Infosys Consultants Pvt. Ltd.

The company began with an initial capital of ₹10,000 borrowed from Murthy's wife. Despite several ups and downs, the company expanded slowly and steadily. In two decades, it became one of the most trusted and largest software companies in the country. By 1999, Infosys had become the first Indian company to be listed on an American stock exchange.

With Murthy at the helm, Infosys became the first listed Indian company with revenues of $1 billion a year. In 2002, Murthy resigned as the CEO of the company after twenty-one years. However, he continued to serve as the chairman and finally retired in 2014. The company designs and delivers technology-enabled business solutions to over 2,000 companies globally. It has close to 1,80,000 employees working in over sixty offices around the world. Murthy played a pivotal role in helping the company flourish and has been described as the 'Father of the Indian IT Sector' by *Time Magazine*.

> *In 1981, Murthy decided to become an entrepreneur again. Along with six other software professionals, he founded a company called Infosys Consultants Pvt. Ltd. The company began with an initial capital of ₹10,000 borrowed from Murthy's wife.*

Industry Leader

Apart from Infosys, Murthy has served as a director on the boards of DBS Bank, Unilever and ICICI. He is also an active philanthropist and serves on the advisory boards and councils of several institutions including Cornell University, Ford Foundation, the UN Foundation and the Indo-British Partnership.

His contributions to the IT sector have earned him numerous recognitions and honours including the prestigious Padma Shri in 2000 and Padma Vibhushan in 2008. He was also awarded the highest French honour, the National Order of the Legion of Honour, in 2008. In 2013, he became the first recipient of the Sayaji Ratna Award, which was established to mark the 151st birth anniversary of Maharaja Sayajirao Gaekwad III, the erstwhile ruler of Baroda. In the same year, he was also named 'Philanthropist of the Year' by the United Kingdom-based Asian Awards.

PRANNOY JAMES ROY

Born on: 15 October 1949

Birthplace: Kolkata, West Bengal

Claim to Fame: Founder of NDTV

'The journalistic talent in India is outstanding. We are more lively, hungry and vibrant. We have just one simple problem and I have been fighting to change that for the credibility and future of news. We just have no punishment for defamation.'

PRANNOY ROY

Journalist

Prannoy James Roy was born to a Bengali father and Irish mother and was an achiever right from a young age. After attending La Martiniere, Kolkata and The Doon School, Dehradun, he received a scholarship to complete his schooling from Haileybury and Imperial Service College in the UK. He then studied economics at the University of London's Queen Mary College and went on to get his PhD from the Delhi School of Economics.

Back in India, Roy worked as an economic advisor in the finance ministry. He was also an associate professor at the Delhi School of Economics, where he developed a macro-econometric forecasting model for the Indian economy. Additionally, he worked as a consultant to the India division of international accountancy firm, PricewaterhouseCoopers.

A renowned psephologist, he studies and scientifically analyses elections. This led him to Doordarshan and BBC World News studios, where he was the lead anchor for budget- and election analysis-based shows.

Changing Indian News

In 1988, along with his wife Radhika, Roy founded New Delhi Television Limited (NDTV). He later created a subsidiary called NDTV 24x7, which became India's first twenty-four-hour English news channel. Roy has hosted many programmes on NDTV, inspiring a generation of journalists and becoming an important part of the evolution of news broadcasting in India. Today, the NDTV network has more than twenty-three studios throughout the length and breadth of the country.

Through NDTV, Roy has also worked on many social awareness campaigns like 'Save Our Tigers', '7 Wonders of India' and 'Greenathon'. One of the campaigns that had a lasting impact on the country was a drive against bribes, which was spread over forty-eight Indian cities with 1,500 volunteers working on the ground to create awareness on fighting corruption.

In 1988, along with his wife Radhika, Roy founded New Delhi Television Limited (NDTV). He later created a subsidiary called NDTV 24x7, which became India's first twenty-four-hour English news channel. Roy has hosted many programmes on NDTV, inspiring a generation of journalists and becoming an important part of the evolution of news broadcasting in India.

Many Talents, Many Awards

Roy has worked with the International Advisory Board of the Council on Foreign Relations in Washington DC, USA. He is also a published author and a certified British chartered accountant.

Over the years, Roy has received many honours and awards in recognition of his work. He was presented the 2015 RedInk Award for Lifetime Achievement for Excellence in Journalism for his consistent and pioneering contribution to news television in India. He was also awarded the Thoppil Gopalakrishnan Memorial Award instituted by the Kerala-based Media Trust in 2009 for excellence in journalism. He has won many other prestigious awards including the B D Goenka Award for excellence in journalism in 1994 and 1995, the Screen Videocon Award for Lifetime Achievement in 1998, the Limca Book of Records Person of the Year award in 1998 and the Ernst & Young - Entrepreneur of the Year Award (Media) in 2003.

SAINT TERESA

26 August 1910 - 5 September 1997

Birthplace: Skopje, Republic of Macedonia

Claim to Fame: Founder of the Order of the Missionaries of Charity

*'Spread love everywhere you go.
Let no one ever come to you
without leaving happier.'*

SAINT TERESA

Social Worker

Saint Teresa was born Agnes Gonxha Bojaxhiu in Skopje, which is now a part of Macedonia. Her father's sudden death when she was about eight years old left her family in dire financial straits. At the age of eighteen, Agnes left her home to join the Institute of the Blessed Virgin Mary, known as the Sisters of Loreto, in Ireland, which had a mission in Kolkata. There she received the name Sister Mary Teresa and in December 1928, she departed for India to arrive in Kolkata on 6 January 1929.

In Kolkata, she started to teach students at the St Mary's School for Girls. On 24 May 1937, Sister Teresa made her Final Profession of Vows, and from then onwards was known as Mother Teresa. She continued teaching at the school and soon became its principal.

Receiving Her Calling

On 10 September 1946, during a train ride from Kolkata to Darjeeling, Mother Teresa decided to establish a religious community called the Missionaries of Charity, which would be dedicated to the service of the poorest of the poor. On 17 August 1948, she left Loreto Convent to begin her life of charity dressed in what would become her trademark white saree with a blue border.

To prepare for her new path, Mother Teresa took a short course with the Medical Mission Sisters in Patna. She returned to Kolkata and found temporary lodging with the Little Sisters of the Poor and on 21 December 1948, she went to the slums for the first time. She visited families, washed the sores of children, cared for an old man lying sick on the road and nursed a woman dying of hunger and tuberculosis, thus beginning a lifelong dedication to serving the destitute.

On 7 October 1950, the new congregation of the Missionaries of Charity was officially established in the Archdiocese of Calcutta. In 1957, she began work with those suffering from leprosy and slowly expanded her educational work, at one point running nine elementary schools in Kolkata. She also opened a home for orphans and abandoned children.

By the early 1960s, Mother Teresa began to send her sisters to other parts of India. Pope Paul VI soon encouraged her to open a house in Venezuela, followed by one each in Rome, Italy and Tanzania and eventually, on every continent. By the 1990s, Mother Teresa had opened houses in almost all of the communist countries around the world, including the Soviet Union.

Less than two years after her death, in view of Mother Teresa's widespread reputation of holiness, Pope John Paul II permitted the opening of her Cause of Canonization. On 20 December 2002, he approved the decrees of her heroic virtues and miracles. In 2016, Agnes Gonxha Bojaxhiu officially became known as Saint Teresa.

In spite of everything she did, Mother Teresa still felt she wasn't doing enough. She formed the Sick and Suffering Co-Workers in 1953 and the Co-Workers of Mother Teresa in 1954. In 1963, she founded the Missionaries of Charity Brothers; in 1976, she founded the Contemplative Branch of Sisters; in 1979, the Contemplative Branch of Brothers; and in 1984, the Missionaries of Charity Fathers.

From Mother to Saint

Over the years, Mother Teresa won numerous awards for her charity work including the Padma Shri in 1962, the Nobel Peace Prize in 1979 and the Bharat Ratna in 1980. Mother Teresa died on 5 September 1997. The government of India gave her a state funeral and her body was buried in the Mother House of the Missionaries of Charity in Kolkata. Less than two years after her death, in view of Mother Teresa's widespread reputation of holiness, Pope John Paul II permitted the opening of her Cause of Canonization. On 20 December 2002, he approved the decrees of her heroic virtues and miracles. In 2016, Agnes Gonxha Bojaxhiu officially became known as Saint Teresa.

SAM HORMUSJI FRAMJI JAMSHEDJI MANEKSHAW

3 April 1914 - 27 June 2008

Birthplace: Amritsar, Punjab

Claim to Fame: First Indian Army officer to be promoted to the rank of field marshal

'A "Yes Man" is a dangerous man. He is a menace. He will go very far. He can become a minister, a secretary or a field marshal but he can never become a leader nor, ever be respected. He will be used by his superiors, disliked by his colleagues and despised by his subordinates. So discard the "Yes Man".'

SAM MANEKSHAW

Army Officer

Sam Hormusji Framji Jamshedji Manekshaw, better known as Sam Manekshaw, was born to Parsi parents in Amritsar. His father, Hormusji Manekshaw was a doctor who had also served as a captain in the Indian British Army. Manekshaw was a brilliant student and studied at the Sherwood College in Nainital. His goal was to be a gynaecologist and he asked his father to send him to England to study medicine when he completed school with flying colours. However, when he was refused permission to travel because his parents thought he was too young, he decided to appear for the entrance examination for the Indian Military Academy (IMA) in rebellion. He soon became one of the first forty cadets to graduate from IMA and was commissioned as a second lieutenant in the British Indian Army, which became the Indian Army after independence.

After partition in 1947, Manekshaw was reassigned to the 16th Punjab Regiment. His long and productive career with the army lasted for forty years, during which time he was part of the Royal Scots, 4/12 Frontier Force Regiment, 8th Gorkha Rifles, Infantry School, 26th Infantry Division, Defence Services Staff College, IV Corps, Western Command and Eastern Command. He fought in World War II as well as in the Indo-Pakistan War of 1947, the Sino-Indian War of 1962, the Indo-Pakistan War of 1965 and the Bangladesh Liberation War of 1971.

Standing His Ground

In April 1971, Indira Gandhi, who was the prime minister of India at the time, asked army chief General Manekshaw if he was ready to go to war with Pakistan. Manekshaw refused, asserting that his single armoured division and two infantry divisions were deployed elsewhere and only thirteen of his 189 tanks were fit to fight. He also pointed out that the Himalayan passes would open up, which would result in heavy flooding. When Indira Gandhi asked the cabinet to leave the room and Manekshaw to stay, he offered to resign.

When the Indian Army finally went to war in December that year, the fortnight-long war brought home 90,000 Pakistani prisoners of war. Pakistan surrendered and Bangladesh was born. When Gandhi asked Manekshaw to go to Dhaka and accept the surrender of Pakistani forces, he declined, saying the honour should go to his army commander in the east, Lieutenant General Jagjit Singh Aurora.

His long and productive career with the army lasted for forty years, during which time he was part of the Royal Scots, 4/12 Frontier Force Regiment, 8th Gorkha Rifles, Infantry School, 26th Infantry Division, Defence Services Staff College, IV Corps, Western Command and Eastern Command.

Sam the Brave

Sam Manekshaw received several awards and accolades for his service to the Indian Army. He was awarded the Military Cross in 1942, the Padma Bhushan in 1968 and the Padma Vibhushan in 1972. In 1972, when he was of retirement age, the president of India asked him to extend his service by six months on special orders. He was reluctant but he complied out of respect. On 1 January 1973, he was conferred the rank of field marshal, the highest attainable rank in the Indian Army. The IMA has named one of its battalions after Manekshaw. He is an inspiration to millions of soldiers and was given the title, 'Sam Bahadur' (Sam the Brave) by the Indian Army's Gorkha Regiment.

SATYENDRA NATH BOSE

1 January 1894 - 4 February 1974

Birthplace: Kolkata, West Bengal

Claim to Fame: Work on quantum mechanics in the early 1920s and association with Albert Einstein

'I have got all the recognition I deserve.'

SATYENDRA NATH BOSE

Scientist

Satyendra Nath Bose was born on 1 January 1894 in Kolkata. Bose's father, Surendranath Bose, was an accountant in the East Indian Railway Company and was deeply interested in mathematics and science. He recognised his son's aptitude for mathematics and would write complicated mathematical sums on the floor for his son to solve.

AN EARLY START TO ACADEMIC EXCELLENCE

Bose was always a brilliant student and finished school with flying colours. Bose went on to study at the Presidency College in Kolkata, where he studied under renowned scientists like Jagadish Chandra Bose and Prafulla Chandra Ray.

After completing his master's degree, Bose became a physics scholar at the University of Calcutta in 1916 and began his research on the theory of relativity. He soon set up new departments and laboratories where new undergraduate and graduate courses were initiated.

In 1921, he was offered the post of reader at the University of Dhaka. There again he helped set up new laboratories to teach advanced courses in science. During this time, he also worked with his former classmate and astrophysicist Meghnad Saha on quantum physics and relativity theory.

ASSOCIATION WITH EINSTEIN

In 1924, Bose wrote a paper on deriving Planck's quantum radiation law. Bose's method was based on the argument that one photon of light is not distinguishable from another of the same colour, which meant that a new way of counting particles was needed. When his work was not accepted for publication, he sent it to Albert Einstein, who having recognised the significance of Bose's findings, collaborated with him. Einstein extended Bose's argument to a wider range of phenomena and together the duo created the Bose-Einstein statistics. Any particle that behaves in accordance with the B-E statistics is classed as a boson, named in honour of Bose.

Einstein extended Bose's argument to a wider range of phenomena and together the duo created the Bose-Einstein statistics. Any particle that behaves in accordance with the B-E statistics is classed as a boson, named in honour of Bose.

After his paper was published, Bose spent two years in Europe working with Einstein and Marie Curie in Germany and France. He returned to Dhaka in 1926, where he became the head of the physics department at the University of Dhaka and designed equipment for an X-ray crystallography laboratory. He also served as the dean of the science faculty at the university until 1945. At the time of India's partition, Bose returned to Kolkata and taught there till 1956.

Awards and Recognition

For his pioneering contributions to science, Bose was honoured with a Padma Vibhushan in 1954, the second-highest civilian honour in India. Five years later, in 1959, he was appointed as the National Professor, the highest honour in the country for a scholar. Bose also became an advisor to the Council of Scientific and Industrial Research as well as president of the Indian Physical Society and the National Institute of Science. About twelve years after Bose's death on 4 February 1974, the Indian government established the S N Bose National Centre for Basic Sciences in Salt Lake, Kolkata.

SHAHEEN MISTRI

Born on: 16 March 1971

Birthplace: Mumbai, Maharashtra

Claim to Fame: Contribution to the upliftment of children from low-income communities

'A good education is one that addresses the needs of the child and the community they live in while still providing a strong set of values that equips them to make better and informed decisions for themselves and their families.'

SHAHEEN MISTRI

Educator

Shaheen Mistri is a well-known educator and social activist. She is the founder of Akanksha Foundation and Teach For India, where she has been the CEO since 2008. Mistri serves on the boards of the Indian School Leadership Institute and Design for Change, a global movement of children. She is also a committee member for the National Council for Teacher Education.

Mistri was born into a Parsi family in Mumbai. Due to her father's transferable job, Mistri and her family moved to thirteen different countries while she was growing up, including the United States, Greece, Lebanon, Indonesia and Saudi Arabia. She attended many different schools but always spent her summer vacations in India.

Passion for Service

During these breaks, Mistri would volunteer at a school for the visually impaired or at an orphanage. Her volunteering was driven by her passion to better the lives of children. She often credits her parents – a banker father and a speech therapist mother – for inculcating such values in her.

During one such vacation in India, following her first year at Tufts University, USA, Mistri learnt that children living in the city's slums lack access to quality education and are deprived of the necessary skills required to lead a normal, fulfilling life. She then decided to quit the university and move back to India to be able to bring about the change she thought was needed.

Birth of Akanksha

Mistri enrolled for a course in sociology at St Xavier's College in Mumbai. Here she convinced a group of college friends to volunteer as teachers and asked the college to let them use empty classrooms after hours. Her efforts paid off and soon the first Akanksha centre was born. Around fifteen children from neighbouring slums attended the first class that Mistri taught.

Over the next twenty-five years, the centre expanded into a foundation with over 4,500 children enrolled in fifty-one centres and sixteen schools across Mumbai and Pune. The teachers and volunteers at Akanksha centres use innovative methodologies to teach and this has won the foundation many prestigious national and international honours.

During one such vacation in India, following her first year at Tufts University, USA, Mistri learnt that children living in the city's slums lack access to quality education and are deprived of the necessary skills required to lead a normal, fulfilling life. She then decided to quit the university and move back to India to be able to bring about the change she thought was needed.

Teaching India

With growing popularity and recognition, Mistri expanded her reach even further when she met Wendy Kopp, the CEO and co-founder of Teach For America. Along with five other colleagues, Mistri launched Teach For India in 2008, with an aim to provide an excellent education to all children and build leaders who are committed to ending educational inequality in the country. Till date, Teach For India has recruited, trained and placed nearly 1,700 fellows in schools across seven cities.

Over the years, Mistri has earned global recognition for her dedication and commitment to the fight for educational equity. She was honoured with the Ashoka Fellow Award in 2001. In 2002, she was named as a Global Leader for Tomorrow at the World Economic Forum and in 2006, she was named as an Asia Society 21 Leader.

VERGHESE KURIEN

26 November 1921 - 9 September 2012

Birthplace: Kozhikode, Kerala

Claim to Fame: Orchestrating the White Revolution in India

'True development is not the development of land, or of cows; it is the development of men and women.'

VERGHESE KURIEN

Dairy Engineer

Verghese Kurien was born on 26 November 1921 in Kozhikode, Kerala. He was the son of Puthen Parakkal Kurien, a civil surgeon. Kurien studied science at Loyola College and obtained an engineering degree from the Guindy College of Engineering, both in Chennai. In 1943, he joined the TISCO Technical Institute as a graduate apprentice and later obtained a scholarship from the government of India to study dairy engineering. After some specialised training at the Imperial Institute of Animal Husbandry and Dairying, Bengaluru, he travelled to the United States to complete his master's degree in mechanical engineering with dairy engineering as a minor subject from Michigan State University in 1948.

OPERATION FLOOD

On his return to India, Kurien was assigned to a government creamery in Anand, Gujarat in 1949. After a short stint there, he decided to quit and move to Mumbai but Tribhuvandas Patel, the then chairman of Kaira District Co-operative Milk Producers Union (now known as Amul), requested him to stay on and help put his co-operative dairy's equipment together. Over time, Kurien held many positions at Kaira. Through his time there, he dedicated himself to empowering farmers through co-operatives. These co-operatives became a model for other companies in India and developing countries across the world.

In 1970, Kurien started Operation Flood, which was also known as the White Revolution. This project was meant to create a flood of milk in India's villages. The project helped to raise India's milk production and has emerged as India's largest rural employment programme. Today, some fourteen million farmers in more than one lakh villages are linked to nearly 180 milk unions spread across twenty-four states of India. The co-operatives established under Operation Flood continue to provide lessons in entrepreneurship and democracy to India's rural people.

From Milk to Oil, Fruits and More

Following the success of the White Revolution, the government brought other primary commodities like edible oils, fruits and vegetables under Kurien's care. In 1979, the Oilseeds Growers' Cooperative Project established a direct link between the producers and consumers of oil, hence reducing the role of oil traders and oil exchanges. This stabilised oil prices, provided an incentive to oilseed growers and reduced India's dependence on oil imports. Kurien also set up Dhara, a company that produces refined oils. In the mid-1980s, he set up a pilot project for the marketing of fruits and vegetables in Delhi. This helped fruit and vegetable growers connect to consumers in Delhi.

In 1970, Kurien started Operation Flood, which was also known as the White Revolution. This project was meant to create a flood of milk in India's villages. The project helped to raise India's milk production and has emerged as India's largest rural employment programme.

In 1988, Kurien facilitated the restructuring of the National Co-operative Dairy Federation of India to provide a national-level body for the country's state-run co-operative dairy federations. He also established Anandalaya Education Society, which provides quality school education to the children of dairy employees in Anand. In 1994, he helped set up Vidya Dairy, which provides modern dairy plant training to senior students graduating in dairy technology.

Kurien's work has received national and international recognition. The government of India awarded him the Padma Shri in 1965, the Padma Bhushan in 1966 and the Padma Vibhushan in 1999. He is also the recipient of the Ramon Magsaysay Award for Community Leadership in 1963, the Carnegie Wateler World Peace Prize in 1986 and the World Food Prize in 1989.

VIKRAM AMBALAL SARABHAI

12 August 1919 - 30 December 1971

Birthplace: Ahmedabad, Gujarat

Claim to Fame: 'Father of the Indian Space Programme'

'He who can listen to music in the midst of noise can achieve great things.'

VIKRAM SARABHAI

Space Scientist

Vikram Ambalal Sarabhai belonged to an affluent family in Gujarat. His father was one of the most respected industrialists of his time and his mother ran a private school. The Sarabhai family was deeply influenced by Mahatma Gandhi and Rabindranath Tagore and took active part in the freedom struggle. Many eminent leaders often visited Sarabhai's home, which helped Sarabhai understand politics and the state of affairs in British India and later, independent India too.

After clearing the intermediate science examination from the Gujarat College in Ahmedabad, Sarabhai moved to the UK. He studied at St John's College in the University of Cambridge but he had to return to India during World War II. Once back, he joined the Indian Institute of Science, Bengaluru to carry out research. After a few years, Sarabhai went back to Cambridge to continue his studies and research on cosmic rays. He then earned his PhD and returned to India to implement his learnings.

Stars in His Eyes

On 11 November 1947, Sarabhai established the Physical Research Laboratory in Ahmedabad. The laboratory started its operations from his residence. Its first research topic was cosmic rays. With his group of students, Sarabhai started setting up cosmic ray telescopes to monitor the changing trends in cosmic radiation and the intensity of cosmic rays in different places like Kodaikanal, Gulmarg and Trivandrum.

Sarabhai's education and research experience prepared him to take on the challenge of initiating India's space programme soon after Russia launched the world's first artificial satellite, Sputnik. He started a project for the fabrication and launch of the first Indian satellite, Aryabhata, which was put into orbit in 1975, after his death. It explored the conditions of Earth's ionosphere and measured neutrons and gamma rays from the sun. The satellite's scientific instruments had to be switched off during its fifth day in orbit because of a failure in the satellite's electrical power system. However, it did manage to gather useful information in its five days of operation.

With support from the government, Sarabhai went on to establish the Indian National Committee for Space Research (INCOSPAR) in 1962 and became its first chairman. In 1969, INCOSPAR was restructured and renamed Indian Space Research Organisation (ISRO) and Sarabhai took on an advisory role here as well. The major objective of ISRO was to advance space technology and apply it for national benefits.

Sarabhai was also responsible for bringing satellite television to India. In fact, it was his communications with NASA that formed the basis for the Satellite Instructional Television Experiment in 1975.

Additionally, Sarabhai served as the chairman of the Atomic Energy Commission and helped set up the first rocket launching station, at Thumba near Thiruvananthapuram. Sarabhai was also responsible for bringing satellite television to India. In fact, it was his communications with NASA that formed the basis for the Satellite Instructional Television Experiment in 1975.

Feet on the Ground

Sarabhai was not only a pioneering scientist, but also a great philanthropist and community leader. He founded a community science centre in Ahmedabad in 1966, which is now called the Vikram A Sarabhai Community Science Centre. He helped give life to the Ahmedabad Textile Industry's Research Association, which helped in the development of textiles across the country; the Indian Institute of Management in Ahmedabad; and Operations Research Group, the first market research organisation in the country. He also founded the Nehru Foundation for Development, which promotes research on problems of development. For his dedication to science and his contributions to society, Sarabhai was awarded the Padma Bhushan in 1966 and the Padma Vibhushan in 1972, posthumously.

ROBINAGE: WEEKLY CHILDREN'S NEWSPAPER

RobinAge is an award-winning weekly newspaper for children aged four to sixteen years. It carries news and information on current affairs, science, history, sports, careers, culture and environment along with activities, puzzles and interactive projects.

Each issue also includes a special *Jr RobinAge* supplement for young readers, which includes fun activities, general knowledge and the Each One Teach One Programme, which children can use to learn and teach basic written and spoken English.

Founded in 2008, *RobinAge* has grown to become a favourite amongst kids, reaching schools and children's homes across India via subscription. The newspaper has also won multiple national and international awards, including three Parents' Choice Awards (USA).

To learn more about *RobinAge,* visit www.robinage.com

ADITYA KRISHNAMURTHY

Aditya Krishnamurthy is a Mumbai-based artist and illustrator. He has been illustrating select children's books since 2016, specialising in a range of styles including line art, pointillism and mixed media techniques like ink and watercolour wash.

Aditya's current art practice involves building a body of work using acrylic on canvas, charcoal and pastel on paper and ink and watercolour wash. His practice also includes commissioned projects. Prior to becoming a full-time artist and illustrator, Aditya was an investment banker working with leading finance firms in Mumbai.

To know more about Aditya's work, contact him via e-mail on ad.krishnamurthy@gmail.com